THE FABULOUS FLYING
FANDINIS!

INGRID SLYDER

COBBLEHILL BOOKS/Dutton
New York

Library of Congress Cataloging-in-Publication Data
Slyder, Ingrid.
The Fabulous Flying Fandinis /
written and illustrated by Ingrid Slyder.
p.   cm.
Summary: Because the new neighbors live in a strange house
and have strange pets, Bobby fears visiting them and hesitates
joining in the fun at their home.
ISBN 0-525-65212-4 (hardcover)
[1. Neighborliness—Fiction.   2. Fear—Fiction.]   I. Title.
PZ7.S6364Fab   1996   [E]—dc20   95-17892   CIP   AC

Published in the United States by Cobblehill Books,
an affiliate of Dutton Children's Books,
a division of Penguin Books USA Inc.,
375 Hudson Street, New York, New York 10014
Typography by Kathleen Westray
Printed in Hong Kong
First edition   10 9 8 7 6 5 4 3 2 1

FOR DUANE

When the Fabulous Flying Fandinis
moved in, the neighbors said
they were strange.
"Strange house," said Mr. Smith.
"Strange pets," said Mrs. Jones.

Bobby Brown lived two doors down.

"The Fandinis are friendly folks," said Mom.

"With lots of children to play with," said Dad.

"No way, forget it," said Bobby. "They could be strange, have cooties, or worse."

But Dad just laughed. "Go on, go see."

Mrs. Fandini answered the door.
"Come in, come in."

Inside, the house had no doors,
nor stairs, nor walls.
Only trapezes.
Trapezes full
of Fabulous Flying Fandinis.

"Jump on! Join in!" the children cried,
as they whizzed above Bobby's head.

"No way," Bobby said.
"I might get a nosebleed, a blister,
or worse."

And when it was evening
the Fandinis
mounted their elephant
and walked
Bobby home.

"So tell us," said Mom,
"did you try something fun?"
"So tell us," said Dad,
"did you try something new?"
"No way," said Bobby.

Next morning
the neighbors shook their heads.
"Strange way to bring in the groceries."

"Come in, come in,"
said Mr. Fandini.
"Just in time
for breakfast."

A tattooed lady
served pancakes on a trampoline.
"Jump on! Join in!" cried the children.
"Not today," Bobby said.
"I might get queasy, lose a tooth,
or much worse."

After breakfast the little Fandinis
took turns bathing.
"Jump on! Join in!" they cried,
as they dove without a splash.

"Forget it," said Bobby.
"I could catch a cold, belly flop,
or much, much worse."

And when evening came they mounted
their unicycles and pulled Bobby home.

"Did you join in?" asked Dad.
"No way," said Bobby. "I might not like it."
"You'll never know unless you try," said Mom.

Next morning
the neighbors scratched their chins.
"Strange way to prune trees."

"Come in, come in," said Mrs. Fandini.
"Just in time to help with the laundry."

"Jump on! Join in!"
 cried the little Fandinis,
 daintily hanging their socks.
"Aw, gee," Bobby said. "I might get
 the hiccups or much, much, MUCH worse."
"Why not try something fun?
 Why not try something new?" asked Mrs. Fandini.
 Bobby looked down at his shoes.
 At last he confessed in a tiny whisper,
"I might look stupid."
 The little Fandinis all spoke at once.
"Not if we show you how—just ask!
 Come on! Hold our hands!"

With a friend holding tight
to his left and his right,

Bobby jumped on
and Bobby joined in.
Hurray! Hurray!

And that night
Bobby went home
by way of the cannon.